Text copyright © 2010 by Barbra Williams

Illustrations copyright © 2010 by David Neal

Library of Congress Cataloging-in-Publication Data

Author: Williams, Barbra

Wendy Worm Meets New Friends

ISBN 9780615365237

[1.Worms, - Fiction, 2. Friendship – Fiction]

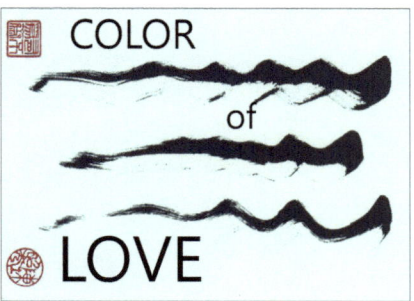

For information regarding permissions, write to Color of Love Publishing Inc.
Attention: Permissions Department, P.O. Box 2168, Sacramento, California 95812

Wendy worm went to the market on such a beautiful day, to buy some treats that were oh- so- sweet, she hurried on her way.

She met a butterfly named Betty sitting and singing a tune. "Betty", she asked. "How are you this fine day in June?"

"Swell," said Betty Butterfly. "Thank you for asking. In this warm afternoon sunlight I'm basking."

"Come join me," said Wendy, "on this fun trip to the marketplace, to buy some treats that are oh- so- sweet, time we must not waste."

So off they went, in quite a hurry, to the market place. When down the path and on the grass, they met a ladybug named Grace.

"It's such a fine day, I should say, where might you two be going?"

"To the market," said Wendy.

"Where the sweet treats are flowing?"

"Would you like to come along with us to the marketplace? With all those sweet treats to eat, we'd better race!"

"Yes, of course," said Grace with a smile and nodding her head up and down. "I love eating sweets and going in to town."

"Hurry," said Wendy. "We must not linger." And back over the hill, she pointed with her finger.

"Straight to the market we must go, before the sun sets low."

Off they went, three very good friends,

on a day so sunny and bright, to buy

some treats that were oh-so sweet and

to be back home by night.

They scooted down the path, on that warm and sunny afternoon. When a duck named Marty appeared, humming his favorite tune. Now, this duck Marty was not quite like the others. He had a rather large beak and his feathers were many colors.

"Stop right there!" he shouted quite loudly. "You're walking in my garden," he pointed out proudly.

"See all those plants growing hardy and strong?"

"To damage and destroy them would just be wrong."

"We are sorry," explained Wendy.

"We're just in a hurry. About destroying your garden, you don't have to worry."

Then said Grace with glee, "The market is where we are going." "Have you heard about how many treats they are showing?"

"Of course", said Marty. "I've heard all about that."

"I've talked about going often with Chester the Cat."

"Would you like to join us," asked Wendy, "on our candy search party?"

"Yes, I'd like that," said the duck named Marty.

"Great," said Wendy. "There's always room for one more."

"A perfect chance," said Marty, "for some sweet treats to score."

A new friend was added to the bunch and off they went for their treats. Each of them hoped they would get enough to eat.

Finally, the market came into view. They could all smell the treats for which their hunger grew.

While eating, they all agreed the treats were so yummy.

They ate so fast that they filled up their tummies.

The friends bought so many treats they had to take them home in a truck, Wendy the worm, Betty the butterfly, Grace the ladybug and Marty the duck.

The story is now over with a lesson to be learned. Friendship is given and sometimes can be earned. For they had each met someone new that they could now call a friend. And they hoped for more adventures and for more time to spend.

The End

www.ingramcontent.com/pod-product-compliance
Lightning Source LLC
Chambersburg PA
CBHW041542240626
47164CB00002B/96